W9-COL-470

For my family

Made in China copyright © Frances Lincoln Limited 2004
Text and illustrations copyright © Deborah Nash 2004

First published in Great Britain in 2004 by
Frances Lincoln Children's Books, 4 Torriano Mews,
Torriano Avenue, London NW5 2RZ
www.franceslincoln.com

Distributed in the USA by Publishers Group West

British Library Cataloguing in Publication Data
available on request

ISBN 1-84507-043-7

Printed in China
1 3 5 7 9 8 6 4 2

Made in CHINA

by Deborah Nash

FRANCES LINCOLN CHILDREN'S BOOKS

Ming lived in a small town in China. One day, his granny made him a paper butterfly and he took it to play in the park. "Look, Paper Butterfly!" he cried. "Look at the dark pine, the twisted rock and the perfect pool. Look at the bamboo all feathery tall..."

Paper Butterfly fluttered her wings happily. But Ming was so excited, he forgot about her and left her behind on a stone.

Bamboo is an important plant in China. It is used for making furniture, paintbrushes and baskets, and in cooking and medicine.

Day after day Paper Butterfly waited for Ming. She felt more and more miserable. Then a dragon came prancing by, with a long twisty body and sparkly scales.

"Nǐ hǎo," he growled.

"Nǐ hǎo," replied the butterfly grumpily.

"You don't look very happy," said the dragon. "What's the matter?"

"I've lost my friend Ming, and I don't know my way home."

Nǐ hǎo means "hello" in Mandarin. Hǎo is pronounced "How".

"I can take you home," said the dragon.
"But first you must answer my question:
what was made in China almost 2,000
years ago and is still
used today?"
"I don't know," replied
Paper Butterfly.
"You'd better find out,"
grinned the dragon.
And away he danced.

The dragon
is a mythical creature.
It is considered very lucky
in China as a bringer
of rain. It was once
the symbol of the Emperor.

Paper Butterfly thought hard about the dragon's question. She flew to the top of a tea pavilion, but all she saw was a tall pagoda. She settled on a peony and pondered some more. Then she went to visit the carp in his perfect pool.

A pagoda is a temple where Buddhist relics and writings are stored.

The Buddhist religion came from India. Buddhists believe that if people treat each other well, there will be universal peace.

They also believe in reincarnation: when people die, their souls are born again in different bodies.

A carp
is a large
goldfish. Fish are
a symbol of plenty
in China.

Paper Butterfly flapped her wings crossly. "No one in this garden knows anything!" she cried. As she flew through the gates, she passed two stone lions. "Nǐ hǎo," she said, but the lions roared so fiercely, they frightened her away.

Lions do not live in China, but they appear in Buddhist art. They are often found standing at gateways guarding entrances to temples and gardens.

Poor lost butterfly! She fluttered down the street looking for an answer to the dragon's question and at last she came to a house with red windows. Inside, she heard people talking.

"They sound happy and helpful," she thought. "I'll ask them."

In China, red is a lucky colour.
It is the colour of joy, life and beauty.

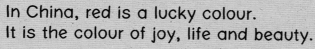

She flew through the red window and found a family eating their lunch. "Nĭ hăo!" she cried. "Nĭ hăo! Nĭ hăo! Nĭ hăo!" But the family were too busy eating and chattering, eating and chattering to answer. They were talking about a heavenly mountain.

As Paper Butterfly listened, she thought, "Surely someone on such a great mountain must know the answer to the dragon's question."

A typical Chinese meal is a bowl of rice with chicken, vegetables, dumplings or noodles, which is eaten using chopsticks. Peking Duck, coated with honey, then roasted and served with pancakes, is a popular dish. The Chinese drink their tea without milk.

It took Paper Butterfly many days to reach the mountain. When she arrived, tired and dusty, she met three wise monkeys.

There are four sacred Buddhist mountains in China. They are Mount Emei, Mount Wutai, Mount Putuo and Mount Jiuhua shan.

One of the monkeys was telling the story of Monkey King, but he took so long to tell it that Paper Butterfly fell asleep without asking her question. When she woke up, all the monkeys had vanished.

Monkey King is a folk character from Buddhist mythology. He stole peaches from the Queen of Heaven's orchard and became immortal.

北京

Off she went again, flying, flying until she reached the great city of Beijing. There she visited the Forbidden City...

Beijing (once called Peking) is the capital of China.
The Forbidden City is a walled palace where the Emperor used to live. In the days when he ruled, ordinary people were not allowed to approach its walls.

... and she followed some bicycles to the Great Wall of China. But no one could tell her the answer to the dragon's question.

The Great Wall of China was built hundreds of years ago to keep the Mongolians out.

So Paper Butterfly flapped her wings and went south. She crossed the Yellow River and came at last to the walled city of Xi'an.

The Yellow River gets its name from the yellow sandy silt it carries, which sometimes makes it flood. The longest river in China is the Yangtze. Xi'an is pronounced "She-an".

She knew that an army of ancient soldiers lived there. People called them "the chocolate soldiers". They were so old, she thought they must know the answer to the dragon's question. But the soldiers stood silently on guard and did not notice Paper Butterfly.

In 1974, some people digging a well uncovered the tomb of Emperor Qin Shihuang. Inside were thousands of life-sized soldiers made of clay. They had been made to guard the Emperor in the afterlife.

"This is hopeless!" thought Paper Butterfly. She stopped to rest at a village decorated with red lanterns and papercuts for the New Year Festival. "I wish I was at home with Ming," she sighed, looking at her torn wings.

At the New Year Festival, families come together to celebrate. They eat a special meal, set off firecrackers and watch dragon and lion dances.

The paper butterfly is a papercut. These are used in villages to decorate windows and doorways during the New Year Festival. Each new year is named after an animal: Rat, Ox, Tiger, Rabbit, Dragon, Snake, Horse, Goat, Monkey, Dog, Cockerel and Pig.

Then, on the window of a house, she noticed another butterfly just like herself, but coloured blue.

"Nĭ hăo," said Paper Butterfly, and she asked the dragon's question one last time.

"That's easy!" exclaimed Blue Butterfly. "We all know what was made in China 2,000 years ago and is still used today. It's . . .

PAP

Paper is thought to have been
invented in 106 AD by Cai Lun,
but new evidence shows that it was
being used in China much earlier.

ER!"

Paper Butterfly fluttered up into the sky with delight. A gust of wind caught Blue Butterfly, tugged her away from the window and carried her up to join Paper Butterfly. Through the clouds came the dragon, twisting and turning towards them.

The two butterflies rode home to Ming on the dragon's back.

In Chinese art, a pair of butterflies is a symbol of love.

Papercuts of a dragon with a phoenix are also symbols of love.

And as they went along, they looked down on the huge, wonderful country of China with all its rivers and mountains, its fields of wheat and rice, its people and bicycles.

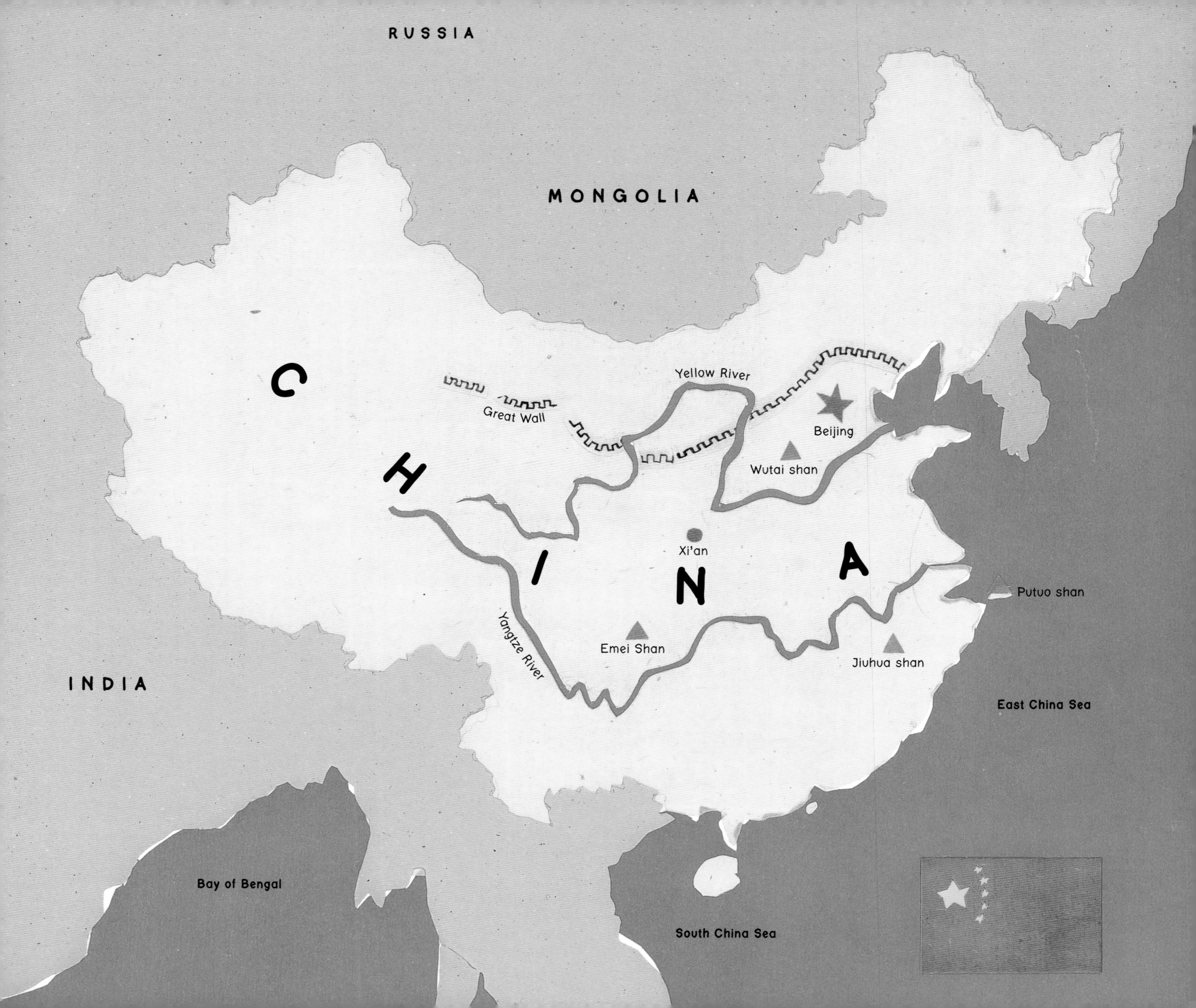
RUSSIA
MONGOLIA
CHINA
Great Wall
Yellow River
Beijing
Wutai shan
Xi'an
Putuo shan
Yangtze River
Emei Shan
Jiuhua shan
INDIA
East China Sea
Bay of Bengal
South China Sea

How to make a Paper Butterfly

1. Fold the red paper square in half.

2. Using a pencil, draw half of Paper Butterfly against the fold.

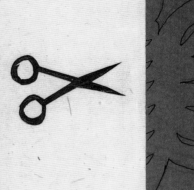

3. Cut the decorative holes out first (get an adult to help you). Then cut out the whole shape.

4. Stick Paper Butterfly on to the white sheet of paper. Using a black pen, draw in the eyes and mouth.

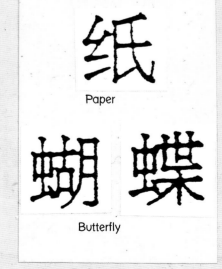

纸

Paper

蝴蝶

Butterfly

5. Practise your Chinese. Write 'Paper Butterfly' in Chinese characters down the page beside Paper Butterfly.